PINKFONG: BABY SHARK AND LITTLE PISCES
A CENTUM BOOK 978-1-912841-91-2
Published in Great Britain by Centum Books Ltd.
This edition published 2019.
1 3 5 7 9 10 8 6 4 2

pinkfong

Centum Books Ltd, 20 Devon Square, Newton Abbot, Devon, TQ12 2HR, UK.

books@centumbooksltd.co.uk

CENTUM BOOKS Limited Reg. No. 07641486.

A CIP catalogue record for this book is available from the British Library.

Printed in China.

pinkfong

BABY SHARK
STORYBOOK SERIES

Baby Shark and Little Pisces

centum

Baby Shark Family & Friends

Baby Shark

Baby Shark is curious about everything under the ocean. He likes singing as it helps him to be brave.

Mummy Shark

Mummy Shark has no limits to what she can do. She always listens to Baby Shark and shares a special bond with him.

Daddy Shark

Daddy Shark is a strong and mighty hunter. More than just a father, he also plays with Baby Shark like a friend.

Little Pisces

Little Pisces falls from a faraway night sky. Even though he sheds lots of tears, he can be brave when he needs to be.

Grandma Shark

Grandma Shark likes reading. A kind and thoughtful grandma, she always has time to spend with Baby Shark.

Grandpa Shark

Grandpa Shark is wise and smart. He is famous for his hot clam buns and enjoys sharing his cooking skills with Baby Shark.

5

Baby Shark wants to play and
is looking for his friends.
'Play with me, play along with me!'

Suddenly, Baby Shark hears a 'boo-hoo' far off in the distance. Baby Shark swims in the direction of the sobs.

'boo-hoo'

Baby Shark finds a twinkling yellow fish crying.
'I am Little Pisces from way up in the sky.
I fell asleep and somehow I fell out of the sky
and into the ocean! Boo-hoo!'

Baby Shark has a really good idea.

'Little Pisces, I think I know how to get you home!'

When Little Pisces hears this, he stops crying.

'Follow me!'

Baby Shark swims off with
Little Pisces right on his tail.

Baby Shark and Little Pisces are on the
wibbly-wobbly ocean see-saw.

'The see-saw can send you up high! I'm sure you'll reach the sky!' says Baby Shark. 'Hooray! I am so excited!' says Little Pisces.

As the see-saw goes 'thump', Little Pisces tries to jump!

But he'll never reach the sky this way.

'Now what?' says Baby Shark.

'I need a long ladder to reach the sky!'
says Little Pisces.
This gives Baby Shark an idea.
'Little Pisces, come this way!'

Baby Shark and Little Pisces find Mr Octopus.
'Mr Octopus has arms that can stretch far and wide!'
says Baby Shark. This makes Little Pisces smile again.
'Wow! Those long arms could reach the sky!'
says Little Pisces.

'Mr Octopus, could you please lift me up to the sky with your long arms?' asks Little Pisces.

'I can stretch my arms tight to their end, but they won't carry you up to the sky, my friend!' explains Mr Octopus. 'But the big whale's spray goes up high, maybe she can get you back to the sky.'

'What can I do? Maybe I can't go back home. . .'
says Little Pisces, as he loses hope.

'Don't worry,' says Baby Shark. 'You'll feel better if we sing a song together.'

'No more tears,
doo-doo-doo-doo-doo!
Spirits high,
doo-doo-doo-doo-doo!'

'My eyes are dry,
doo-doo-doo-doo-doo!
Home is sky,
doo-doo-doo-doo-doo!'

As they sing along together,
they start to feel strong again!

It's the big whale, she can send up a stream of air!

'Hello big whale, I need to reach the sky.

I know your blowhole creates a spray.

Can you help to save the day?' asks Little Pisces.

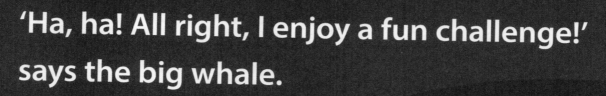

'Ha, ha! All right, I enjoy a fun challenge!' says the big whale.

Little Pisces and Baby Shark jump onto the big whale's back.

WHOOSH!

'Hold tight, here we go!'
The big whale zooms up to the surface!

The big whale shoots a strong stream of air out from her blowhole. Little Pisces and Baby Shark soar high up into the sky!

Wow!

Finally, Little Pisces is reunited with his mum!
Now Baby Shark can say goodbye to his new
friend and return home too.

'Farewell, Little Pisces,
visit again!'

'Thanks for your help big whale!'